American edition published in 2018 by Andersen Press USA,
an imprint of Andersen Press Ltd.
www.andersenpressusa.com

First published in Great Britain in 2018 by Andersen Press Ltd.,
20 Vauxhall Bridge Road, London SW1V 2SA.

Distributed in the United States and Canada by
Lerner Publishing Group, Inc.
241 First Avenue North
Minneapolis, MN 55401 USA
For reading levels and more information, look up this title at www.lernerbooks.com.

Printed and bound in China.

Library of Congress Cataloging-in-Publication Data Available
ISBN: 978-1-5415-1454-6
eBook ISBN: 978-1-5415-1464-5
1-TL-8/1/17

THE WEAVER

Qian Shi

Andersen Press USA

All spiders lead a life of adventure.

Once they are born, they wave goodbye to each other and hitch a ride on the wind.

When the wind drops them off, they set about weaving a web.

Stanley has found
his perfect spot.

Stanley is a weaver, he is also a collector. He collects seeds,

twigs, leaves . . .

and all kinds of precious things
he cannot name.

Stanley is very proud of his collection.

But then the rain comes.

Suddenly,
his home collapses!

He only manages to save one leaf.

How can Stanley keep his leaf safe?

Although he ties it tightly . . .

the wind takes his last leaf away.

Stanley has lost everything.   Hasn't he?

He weaves through the night.

In the morning . . .

it is time for Stanley to
hitch a ride on the wind again.